THE MAGIC FLUTE

The

MUSIC BY

ADAPTED AND ILLUSTRATED BY

Magic Flute

Wolfgang Amadeus Mozart

John Updike and Warren Chappell

New York: Alfred·A·Knopf

*Tamino Cries
for Help*

L. C. catalog card number: 62-18762

THIS IS A BORZOI BOOK, PUBLISHED BY ALFRED A. KNOPF, INC.

Text Copyright © 1962 by John Updike.
Illustrations Copyright © 1962 by Warren Chappell.

ONG AGO to the land of Egypt a handsome young prince named Tamino came wandering. This land was strange to him, and he was alone. Cautiously he entered a deep valley filled with dark rocks. Suddenly the sand whispered, and a great horned snake appeared in his path. It was a dragon! Tamino shot all his arrows, one by one, but they broke on the dragon's scales like chalk. The dreadful monster raised its green head high. Laughter and fire leaped together from its mouth with a noise like crackling cinders.

There was nothing to do but run. Tamino ran and ran, but the dragon's breath grew warmer and warmer upon his heels. At last he could run no further.

"Help! Oh, help!" he cried. "Heavenly gods, have mercy!" The poor prince fell down in a faint. The dragon opened wide his smiling jaws to devour him.

Here our story would end if three veiled maidens had not appeared out of nowhere, waving shining silver swords. Quickly they cut the unlucky dragon in two! This brave deed done, they looked down at Tamino where he lay unconscious on the ground.

"How delicate and beautiful he is!" the first maiden exclaimed, blushing a little.

"Yes, beautiful enough to be a picture," said the second maiden, pursing her lips.

"We must hasten and tell our queen," the third maiden said. She was the sensible one.

"You two go," the first maiden offered. "I will stay here and watch over him."

"No, no," said the second one. "I will stay with him. You two go and tell the queen."

"We will *all* go," the third maiden sensibly decided. So all three went off to tell their queen, leaving the handsome young prince lying where he had fallen.

WHEN Tamino awoke, he discovered the dead dragon by his side. He did not understand. What had happened? Why had he not been eaten? His bewilderment increased as a fat man, dressed all in feathers and bearing on his back a tall birdcage, popped up from behind a hill. This fat man sang in a loud, jolly voice:

"Oh, I am a birdcatcher merry and gay!
I catch silly birds for eight hours a day!
But what I would rather, if I had my wish,
Would be to catch girls, for girls are my dish!

I'd catch them by dozens in dozens of nets,
And feed them with kisses and make them my pets;
The one I loved best, I would make her my wife
And sing her to sleep for the rest of my life!

"Who are you?" Tamino asked in surprise.

"Papageno," the strange man replied, patting his feathers proudly. "I catch birds for the Queen of the Night."

"The Queen of the Night?"

Birdcatcher's Song

"*Shhhh.*" Papageno looked all around. "She rules this land. She is very powerful. Why have you come into her domain?"

Tamino explained, "Dream voices have led me here; for months I have been wandering, seeking I know not what. Today it seemed death was my fate, but a giant must have rescued me."

"Giants? There are no giants here in this land. There are only women, except for me."

"Then," Tamino said, giving the feathery man a grateful hug, "it must have been you who killed this dragon!"

"What dragon?" Papageno asked. He looked down, and at the sight of the monstrous body, his face turned as white as an owl's belly. But when he saw that the dragon was truly dead, he told Tamino boldly, "Yes, I did. I killed this little green snake. It was no trouble at all."

Meanwhile, the three maidens had returned. When they heard Papageno tell this lie, they seized him and set a golden padlock on his mouth.

"Who are *you*?" Tamino asked the maidens.

"We are the servants of the Queen of the Night," they explained. "It was we who slew the dragon and saved your life. We have been to tell the Queen, and she has sent you as a gift this picture of Pamina, her daughter." And they showed Tamino a portrait of a girl so beautiful that his bones turned airy and his blood swirled.

"Oh!" he cried from his heart, "if only this girl were here before me, I would press her to my breast, and she would be mine forever!"

Tamino Sings of Pamina's Beauty

No sooner had he said these words than the clouds thundered and parted to show the Queen of the Night herself, sitting on a glittering throne.

She descended and said to Tamino, "Do not tremble, my son. You are innocent and fair, and perhaps you have been sent to comfort a mother's troubled heart. For my daughter has been stolen from me by a wicked wizard whose name is Sarastro. If you can rescue Pamina from this villain, she will be yours forever."

The Queen Tells of Her Sorrow

"I will, I will!" Tamino cried eagerly.

"Here, then," the Queen said. "Take this magic flute. With it you can rule the moods of men and beasts alike. Whenever it is played, the sad become joyful, the angry become gentle, old men fall in love, and even wild animals are charmed." And she handed the young prince a beautiful flute made all of gold, yet light as a feather; as bright as the sun, yet cool to the touch.

Tamino said, "I hope I can be worthy of such a splendid gift."

"A stout heart," she said, "and a clear mind are a thousand times more precious than gold."

Everyone had forgotten poor Papageno, who was running in little circles saying, "Hm, hm," because he could not move his lips.

Hm, Hm

The Queen ordered that the padlock be removed from his mouth. "Never lie again," she told him sternly. "Now I command you to be Tamino's companion. Go with him to Sarastro's castle."

Papageno protested, "But who will catch birds for you?"

The Queen of the Night said angrily, "My daughter is the bird you must catch. My palace without her is like an empty cage."

He cried, "But Sarastro will have me plucked and roasted and then will feed me to the dogs!"

She smiled and said, "I will give you this to protect you." And she held out a lovely set of bells, with voices so pure they could be heard in a blizzard, through a battle, or at the bottom of the sea.

"Now, go," the Queen said. "My pages will lead you to the castle where my daughter is cruelly kept prisoner. Do not return without her." The sky grew damp and ominous, a black wind blew out of the north, and the Queen of the Night vanished. This was the way things happened in this strange and musical land.

As the three pages led the way to the castle, they sang the two adventurers a song to keep their courage up.

> *"Golden flute and silver bell,*
> *They will keep you very well,*
> *They will bring you home again.*
> *Be brave! Be good! Be men!*
> *Farewell!"*

Then they too vanished, with a soft whistle like wind passing through a keyhole.

TAMINO and Papageno were left alone before the castle of Sarastro. Tamino had expected it to be black and ugly; but instead it was a white and wide and shining temple. He found himself trembling more than ever. It seemed to him that this temple had appeared many times in his dreams. He went to the high bronze door, under a carved sun, and knocked. *Rap rap, rap rap rap.*

From within the marble walls, a huge voice cried, "Stand back!"

Tamino stepped back, and the mysterious voice called again, "What do you seek here?"

"Love and virtue's true reward," Tamino answered. "I seek revenge on the scoundrel Sarastro."

The door opened. There stood a very old man, dressed in the purple robe of a priest. His face held a hundred wrinkles, and his white beard touched his toes. "There is no scoundrel here," he said quietly. "This is the Temple of Wisdom."

"Does Sarastro live here?"

"Yes, Sarastro rules here."

"He is a villain! I hate him with all my heart!" cried the prince.

The old priest smiled. "Why do you say this?"

"An unhappy woman, the Queen of the Night, told me so."

The old priest's smile broadened, and the hundred wrinkles of his face became two hundred. "Women!" he said. "They chatter and chatter because their tongues are like birds. You must let Sarastro explain everything."

"Never!" Tamino said. "He stole the beautiful Pamina from her mother. Where have you hidden her?"

The old priest smiled the third time but answered not a word and closed the door.

Fear, confusion, and sorrow filled Tamino's heart. He turned to Papageno and discovered that Papageno had run away. Tamino was alone; rocks and trees and sand and sky were the only things he could see. Was there no help anywhere? He remembered his magic flute and raised it to his lips to play. It seemed to sing all of itself, and as it sang, animals crept from the forest and sat all around Tamino—all kinds of animals: lions and lizards, monkeys and mice, antelopes and elephants and elegant ostriches, otters, giraffes, geese,

and goats. Even worms came up through the ground to listen, and hawks dropped down from the sky. And the hawks did not eat the worms, and the elephants did not step on the geese. All was harmony.

Hark! Tamino heard from afar a sound of chimes, as pure and clear as water and ice. It was Papageno! His fat friend, feathers flying, came toward him, and with him was another person. This other person was a girl. Her hair was black. Her dress was yellow. Her bracelets were gold and her face—her face was the lovely face of the girl in the portrait.

"It is she!" Tamino cried.

"It is he!" Pamina cried, for Papageno had told her of the handsome prince who had been sent to rescue her.

Like magnet to magnet, or like two clapping hands, the prince and princess rushed gladly toward each other. But from within the temple there arose a clangorous, terrible chant: "LONG LIVE SARASTRO! LONG MAY HE LIVE!"

Papageno sobbed, "Oh, I wish I were a mouse! I wish I were a snail! Then I could creep into my house." And he hid his face in his feathers.

Sarastro himself emerged from the temple. He had a very broad

face, a radiating beard, and a voice like little tumbles of thunder. He spoke very gently. "Do not be afraid," he told them. "I know what is in your hearts."

"Then give me my freedom," Pamina said, "And let me return to my mother."

"Your mother is a proud woman," Sarastro said. "A man must guide your heart. A woman without a man is not complete."

"Then give her to *me*," Tamino said.

"My son," Sarastro said, "you are not yet a man. To show your fitness to marry, you must first pass three tests. These are the tests of faith, of patience, and of courage." Pamina was taken away by the slaves of Sarastro, and Tamino and Papageno were led into a dungeon for the tests of manhood.

First, they were forbidden to speak to any woman. No sooner were they left alone than the three maidens who served the Queen of the Night sneaked into their dungeon.

"What are you doing in this terrible place?" the first maiden asked.

"I have no idea," Papageno answered. "Please get me out."

"Papageno, be quiet," Tamino said. "Remember your vow."

"These priests are wicked men," the second maiden said.

"They are indeed," Papageno said. "I am hungry and miserable."

"Papageno, keep still," Tamino said. "Pay no heed to idle female chattering."

Though the three maidens tried every trick they knew, they could not get Tamino to speak to them. At last the third maiden, the sensible one, said to the others, "We are defeated; let us go." And away they went to report their failure to the Queen.

The priests appeared and praised Tamino for keeping his vow of silence. But Papageno they scolded and sent from the temple. As he wandered about in the wilderness outside, he played to himself on his bells and sang:

> "*Alas, Papageno, if I had a bride,*
> *I would be as wise as the ocean is wide;*
> *The fish in the ocean are happily paired,*
> *But I am alone, and hungry, and scared!*"

Papageno Wishes
for a Bride

A LITTLE old woman popped up in front of Papageno.

"Who are you?" he asked.

"My name is Papagena," she said.

"How strange!" he exclaimed. "My name is Papage*no*."

"I know," she said. "I have come in answer to your song. If you promise to be faithful and kind and to catch many birds to sell so our children may eat, I will promise to marry you."

Papageno was astonished by such boldness. He had desired a pretty young wife like a dove, and this witch was very old and homely. But he remembered how lonely his life had been and decided that an ugly wife was better than no wife at all.

"Oh, all right," he said. "I will marry you." He shook his silver bells to celebrate, and the old woman turned into a lovely girl dressed all in feathers just like him!

How delighted Papageno was! He prepared to give Papagena a kiss. But his life never ran smoothly. Sarastro's priests, still trying to make him wise, appeared and dragged him away to the second test. This was the test of patience. Tamino and Papageno were seated at a long table full of delicious food and drink. Papageno was so happy to see food that he ate with both hands and spilled grape juice all over the tablecloth and stuffed an entire plum into his mouth. The priests, shaking their heads sadly, dragged him away again.

Tamino, on the other hand, ate very neatly and moderately. When he was done, he sat quietly and played upon his magic flute to aid his digestion. Pamina, hearing the familiar song of the flute, crept softly out of her room and came to Tamino in the dining hall. But because he had promised not to speak to any woman, he did not speak to her. Poor Pamina, thinking he no longer loved her, went away with tears streaming down her petal-pale cheeks.

*Pamina Laments
Love's Loss*

Once her mother had given her a little dagger with which to protect herself. Now she prepared to plunge the dagger into her own heart. Its cold point touched her warm skin. She looked toward Heaven for the last time.

"STOP!" a deep voice called, and it was Sarastro. "Foolish child," he said, "it is no time to despair. You have proven great love. Now only one test remains."

This was the test of courage. Tamino had proven his faith and his patience. He was brought before Sarastro. Seeing Pamina, his heart leapt. Remembering his vow of silence, he asked Sarastro, "May I speak to her?" For without his knowing it, his heart no longer served the Queen of the Night, but instead revered Sarastro as a father.

"You may speak to her," Sarastro said.

"Pamina!" he cried. "I always yearned to speak!"

"Tamino!" she answered. "Not death itself will part us now. I will be everywhere at your side; we shall lead each other, and love will lead us both."

They held hands and faced the test of courage together. The gates of the central room of the Temple of Wisdom, the Chamber of Perfect Happiness, flew open. But a wall of fire seemed to bar their way. Tamino lifted the magic flute to his lips. It sang:

"Go, walk by music's might
Through death's enduring night
With gladness, free of fright!"

The waves of flame parted like the wings of a curtain. Tamino and Pamina together passed through unharmed. Their duet of joy rang through the temple, and Sarastro and his priests joined in the chorus. Tamino had become a man, and to this man had been joined a woman, Pamina. Heaven itself rejoiced.

The Chorus of Triumph

And what of Papageno? Poor Papageno, who had failed all his tests, wandered forlornly outside the temple walls. He would never be wise. Slowly, he plucked his feathers one by one, wove a noose of them, and prepared to hang himself from a tree. A bird on a branch called to him, "Think of your bells! Your magic bells!"

"Ah, what good can they do now?" Papageno sighed. Nevertheless, he rang them. How pretty their tinkling was, and how sad!

The Bells Ring

To his surprise, the bird on the branch became Papagena, his own beautiful bride!

"Why, hello!" Papageno said. He suddenly felt quite shy.

Papagena smiled. "How have you been?"

"Terrible. Terrible," Papageno readily told her. "They wouldn't let me talk, or eat, so I made a big fist and I slew them all!"

"My wonderful man!" Papagena cried in delight. Indeed, her delight was so sincere that Papageno felt ashamed.

"Actually," he said, "I didn't slay anybody. I'm just a simple birdcatcher, and somewhat cowardly."

"I know," Papagena said. "But you are still my wonderful man."

Papageno's face brightened. "Truly? You don't despise me?"

"Of course not," replied Papagena. "I would rather marry you than marry Sarastro himself."

The Bird Couple Dances

Papageno shuddered. "Sarastro! I cannot stand to look at his face. He is great, but he is hard."

"Sarastro is hard," Papagena said, "because the world is hard."

"But when I am with you," Papageno told her, taking her hand, "the world seems as soft to me as a pillow of chickadee feathers!" Prancing and fluffing and pecking each other, they sang this song:

"Can this be real? Is this a dream?
The gods are better than they seem,
The foolish, too, are granted bliss!
So come, Papageno,
Come, Papagena,
Pa pa pa pa pa pa pa pa, kiss, kiss, kiss!"

AND what of the Queen of the Night? She, seeing her daughter lost to her forever, became insane with fury. She organized her maidens and slaves into an army and tried to storm and destroy the Temple of Wisdom itself. But her army melted before the might of Sarastro as evening dew melts with the coming of the golden sun. For there is nothing in the world stronger than goodness and truth. The Queen of the Night was not a wicked woman but she was a woman whose will had not yet been subdued to the will of a man. Therefore she was like a proud ship sailing through a tempest without a captain, at the mercy of every wave and wind, all her sails fluttering. Some say, indeed, that in time Sarastro tamed her fierce spirit with patient advice and harmonious music. Perhaps in time they were married. Perhaps Tamino played the magic flute at the wedding. There are more fantastic things than this that are true.